MY HANDS WERE MADE FOR

HELPING

BY: JACQUELYN STAGG

Published and written by Jacquelyn Stagg

ISBN: 978-1-7751833-3-4

Copyright © 2018 by Jacquelyn Stagg

www.jacquelynstagg.com

Dedicated to my mother.

Hi, I'm Charlie and I love to be a helping hand!

"You will discover that you have two hands.
One is for helping yourself and the other is for helping others."

When my mother is working in the garden,

I help by watering the plants so that they can grow!

My hands were made for helping!

When we walk to the park,

I help by holding my sisters hand across the street!

My hands were made for helping!

"No act of kindness, no matter how small, is ever wasted."

AESOP

When we go shopping for groceries,

I help by picking out an extra can of food to donate!

My hands were made for helping!

"No one has ever become poor by giving."

ANNE FRANK

When I have toys that I no longer use,

I help by giving them to kids who don't have as many!

My hands were made for helping!

When my father is folding laundry,

I help by matching all of the socks into pairs!

My hands were made for helping!

"Think of giving not as a duty, but as a privilege."

JOHN D. ROCKEFELLER

When it is time to eat dinner,

I help by setting the table and filling our water glasses!

My hands were made for helping!

When we are finished eating dinner,

I help by making sure that our dog has dinner too!

My hands were made for helping!

"with great power comes great responsibility."

VOLTAIRE

When my mother tucks me in at night,

she always thanks me for being a helping hand!

My hands were made for helping!

"You must be the change you wish to see in the world."

MAHATMA GANDHI

A NOTE FROM THE AUTHOR:

I would like to thank my readers from the bottom of my heart for your on-going support. Every time that you purchase a book from an independent author, an actual person *(me)* does a happy dance!

If you have enjoyed reading this book as much as I have enjoyed writing it, please consider taking a few moments to leave a quick review on ***Amazon.com***.

Stay kind,

Jacquelyn Stagg

www.jacquelynstagg.com

The **Play KIND Initiative** is a new program that we have created as a way to give back to our community, and simply help teach our daughter different and tangible ways to be kind! Together as a family, we will decide where, and how we can be the biggest help by using a portion of our previous month's profits from this book!

**Do you know a child who could benefit
from the Play KIND Initiative?**

Please get in touch.

www.jacquelynstagg.com/playkind

Kindness BINGO

Use this BINGO style Kindness Game to help encourage your child to practice simple, yet powerful acts of kindness!

FREE DOWNLOAD

www.jacquelynstagg.com/kindbingo

KINDNESS CHALLENGE

Conversation starters to help find moments
of kindness in your child's life!

SAYING
SORRY

BEING
POLITE

TAKING
TURNS

BEING A
HELPING
HAND

INCLUDING
EVERYONE

SHOWING
RESPECT

Made in the USA
Coppell, TX
25 October 2019